MAMA AFRICA!

How MIRIAM MAKEBA
Spread Hope with Her Song

KATHRYN ERSKINE

Illustrated by
CHARLY PALMER

FARRAR STRAUS GIROUX / New York

Special thanks to Thando Njovane for her thoughtful consultation on issues of trauma, representation, and South African heritage present in this book.

Farrar Straus Giroux Books for Young Readers
An imprint of Macmillan Publishing Group, LLC
175 Fifth Avenue, New York, NY 10010

mackids.com

Library of Congress Cataloging-in-Publication Data

Names: Erskine, Kathryn author. | Palmer, Charly illustrator.
Title: Mama Africa! : how Miriam Makeba spread hope with her song / by
    Kathryn Erskine ; illustrations by Charly Palmer.
Description: First edition. | New York : Farrar Straus Giroux, 2017 |
    Includes bibliographical references.
Identifiers: LCCN 2016057828 | ISBN 9780374303013 (hardcover)
Subjects: LCSH: Makeba, Miriam—Juvenile literature. | Singers—South
    Africa—Juvenile literature. | Anti-apartheid activists—South
    Africa—Biography—Juvenile literature. | LCGFT: Biographies.
Classification: LCC ML3930.M29 E77 2017 | DDC 782.42163092 [B]—dc23
LC record available at https://lccn.loc.gov/2016057828

Our books may be purchased in bulk for promotional, educational, or business use.
Please contact your local bookseller or the Macmillan Corporate and Premium Sales Department
at (800) 221-7945 ext. 5442 or by e-mail at MacmillanSpecialMarkets@macmillan.com.

*With gratitude to
Zenzile Miriam Makeba
and my mother,
who encouraged me to dance
to her music
—K.E.*

*For my mother, Irma Walker;
my children; and
my grandchildren
—C.P.*

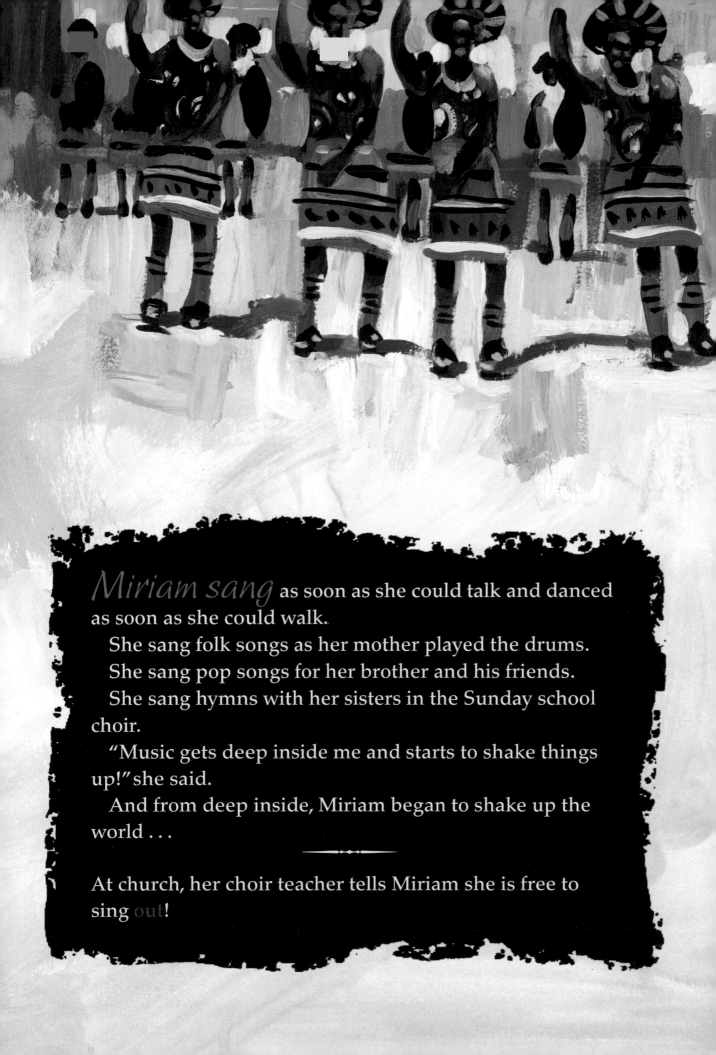

Miriam sang as soon as she could talk and danced as soon as she could walk.

She sang folk songs as her mother played the drums.

She sang pop songs for her brother and his friends.

She sang hymns with her sisters in the Sunday school choir.

"Music gets deep inside me and starts to shake things up!" she said.

And from deep inside, Miriam began to shake up the world . . .

———

At church, her choir teacher tells Miriam she is free to sing out!

CAUTION BEWARE OF NATIVES

R USE BY WHITE

R GEBRUIK DEUR BLANKES

WHITE AREA

BLANKE GEBIED

But out in the world, Miriam is not free. Unless people have white skin, they are not free. Police raid their homes. Sometimes they are arrested. Sometimes they never return. To the baases—the white people who rule South Africa—Miriam's people are just "Bantus."

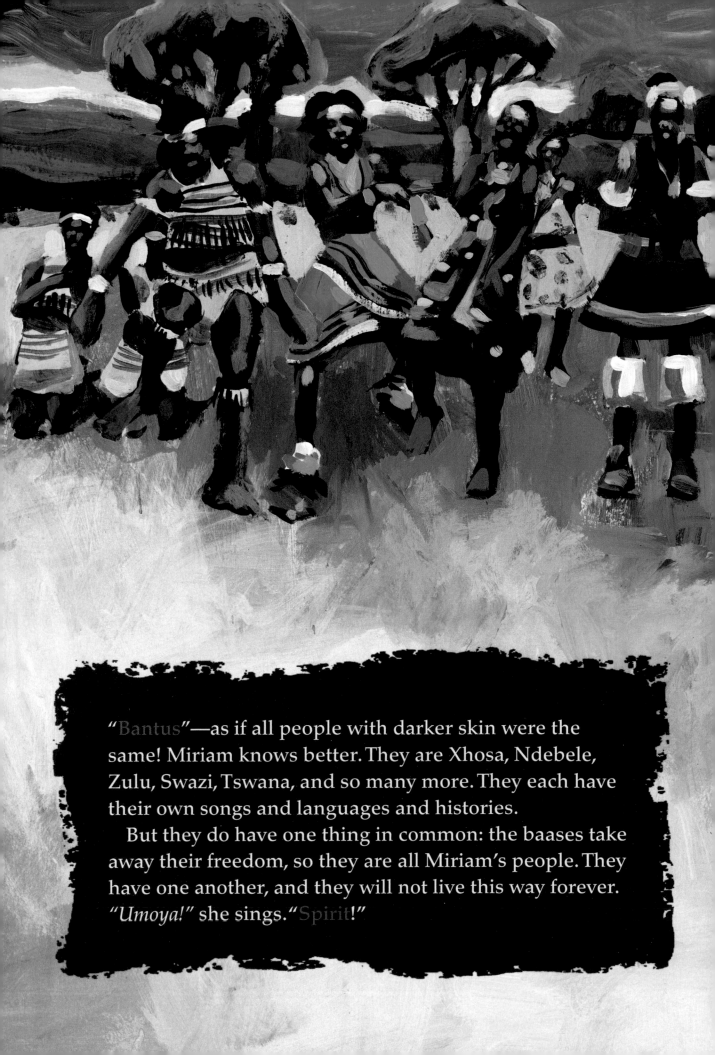

"Bantus"—as if all people with darker skin were the same! Miriam knows better. They are Xhosa, Ndebele, Zulu, Swazi, Tswana, and so many more. They each have their own songs and languages and histories.

But they do have one thing in common: the baases take away their freedom, so they are all Miriam's people. They have one another, and they will not live this way forever. "Umoya!" she sings. "Spirit!"

The Bantu spirit must be broken, the baases decide. They pass even harsher laws of "apartheid" to keep the races separate, crushing the rights of black people and trying to silence their voices.

But Miriam's voice will not be silenced. She goes to the big city, Johannesburg, and sings—even protest songs—in IsiXhosa, IsiZulu, Setswana, and more, because the baases don't understand those languages. It is risky. But Miriam has listened to the protest songs of American singers like Billie Holiday and Ella Fitzgerald, and she feels brave.

"Who can keep us down as long as we have our music?"
Miriam asks. Bravely, she sings out. Like a nightingale.
Soon she is so popular that everyone wants to hear her.

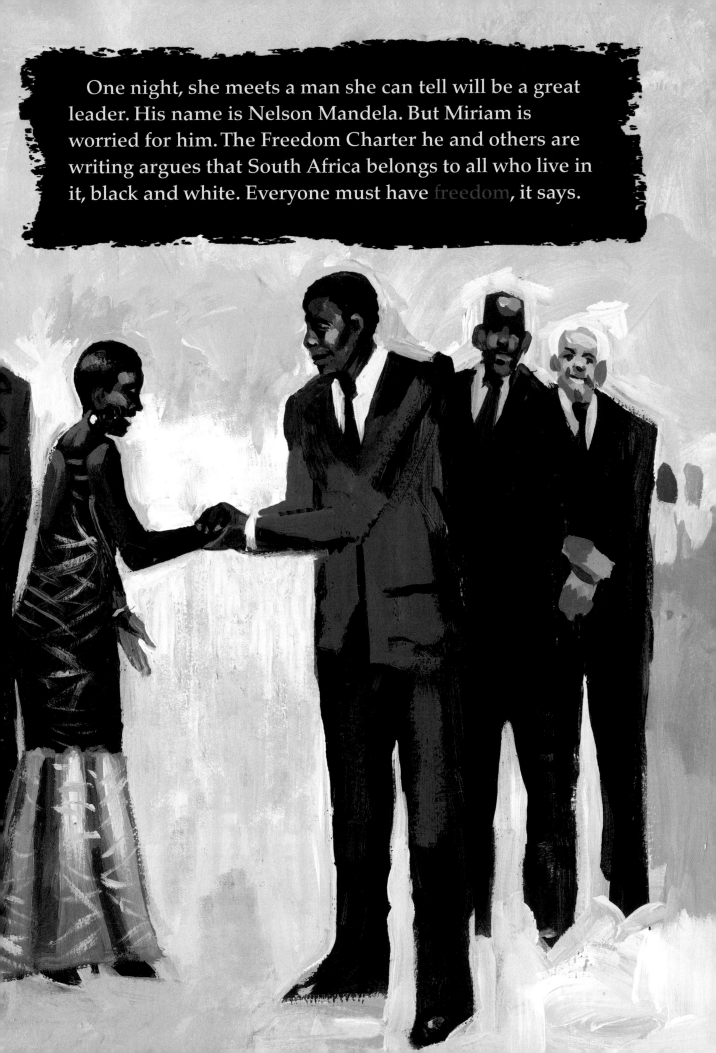

One night, she meets a man she can tell will be a great leader. His name is Nelson Mandela. But Miriam is worried for him. The Freedom Charter he and others are writing argues that South Africa belongs to all who live in it, black and white. Everyone must have freedom, it says.

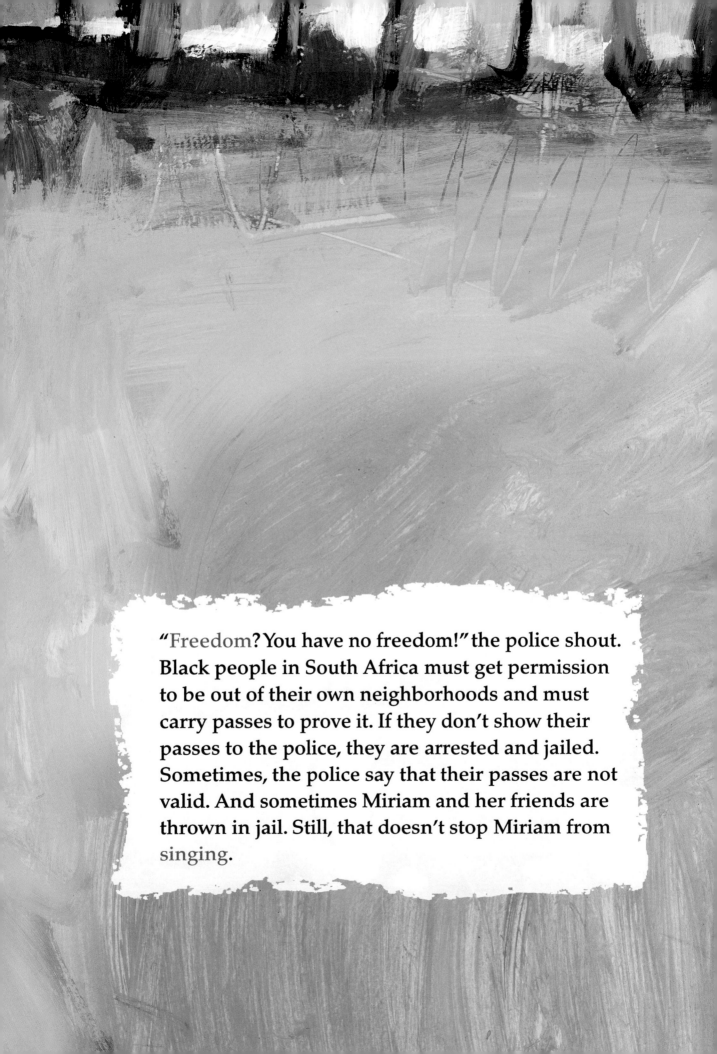

"Freedom? You have no freedom!" the police shout. Black people in South Africa must get permission to be out of their own neighborhoods and must carry passes to prove it. If they don't show their passes to the police, they are arrested and jailed. Sometimes, the police say that their passes are not valid. And sometimes Miriam and her friends are thrown in jail. Still, that doesn't stop Miriam from singing.

Singing always gives her strength. But one night, as she and her group drive home from a concert, there is a terrible crash. Miriam and her friends are hurt, one of them very badly. They need help.

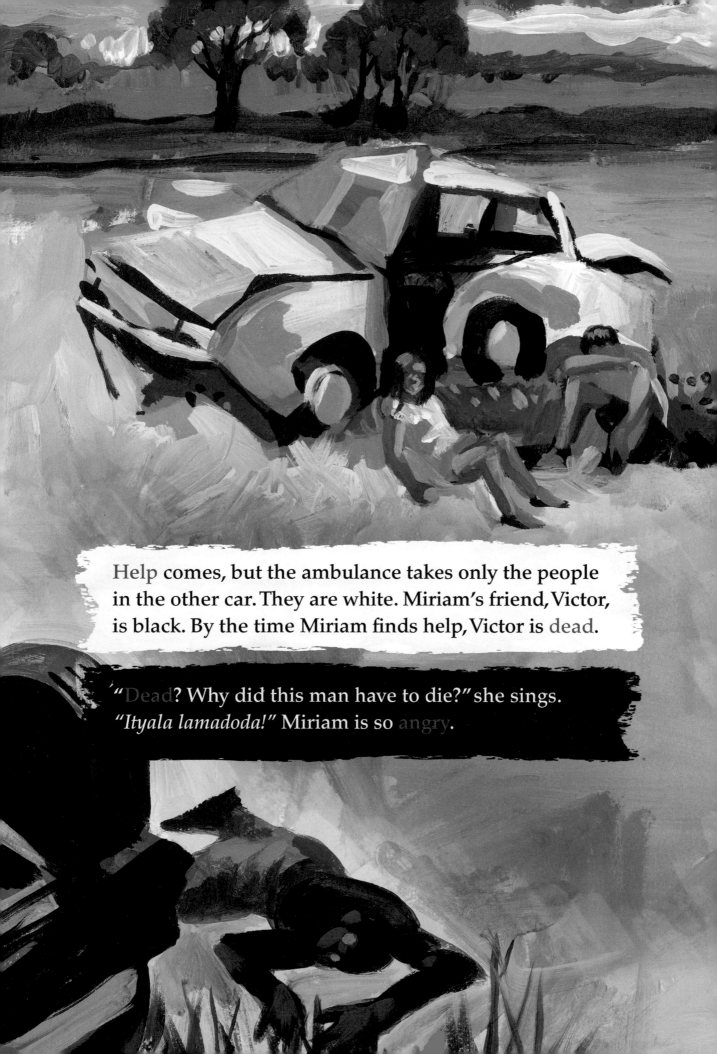

Help comes, but the ambulance takes only the people in the other car. They are white. Miriam's friend, Victor, is black. By the time Miriam finds help, Victor is dead.

"Dead? Why did this man have to die?" she sings. "Ityala lamadoda!" Miriam is so angry.

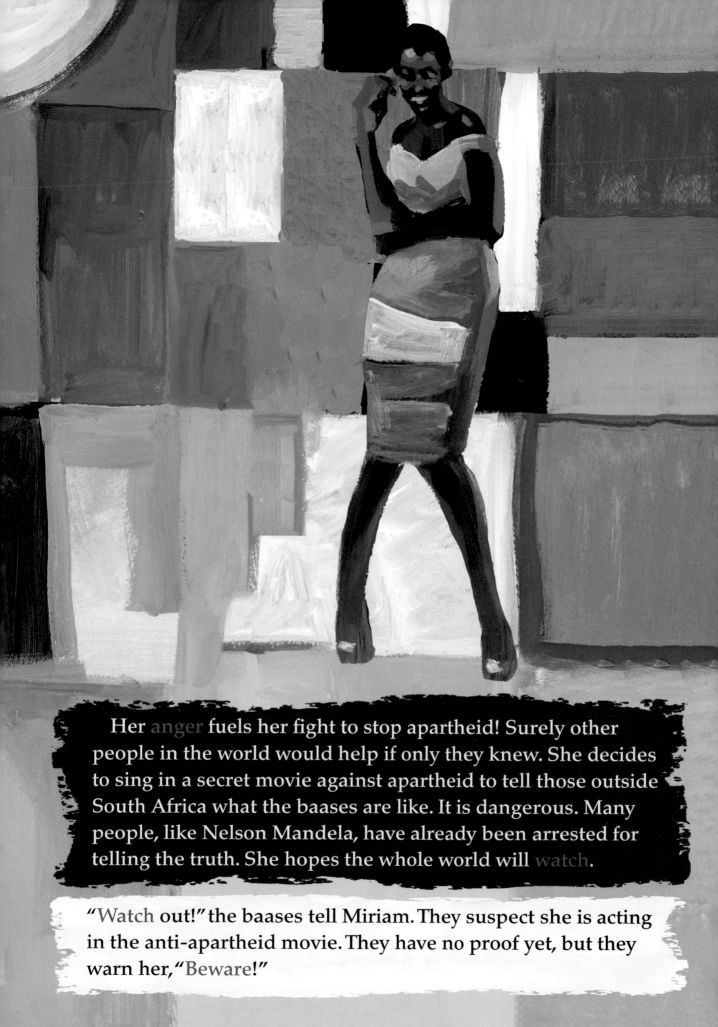

Her anger fuels her fight to stop apartheid! Surely other people in the world would help if only they knew. She decides to sing in a secret movie against apartheid to tell those outside South Africa what the baases are like. It is dangerous. Many people, like Nelson Mandela, have already been arrested for telling the truth. She hopes the whole world will watch.

"Watch out!" the baases tell Miriam. They suspect she is acting in the anti-apartheid movie. They have no proof yet, but they warn her, "Beware!"

"Beware, Verwoerd!" she sings back to the prime minister. *"Ndodemnyama!"* To escape South Africa, Miriam disguises herself in a nanny uniform and boards a plane bound for Europe. For the first time in her life, she is free of apartheid! She sings in London and Los Angeles and New York about what the baases are doing to her people.

But she cannot sing too loudly. Her whole family is still in South Africa. What will the baases do to her people back home?

"Home? South Africa is no longer your home," the baases tell her. If she ever tries to return to her country, they will put her in jail. Even when she finds out her mother is sick, the baases will not let her back in.

In tears, Miriam sings. "*Senzeni na? What have we done?*" She knows her people have done nothing to deserve what the baases do to them. She stays in America and turns her tears into songs against the baases.

The baases pass more laws to stop people from protesting. They arrest thousands and jail many. Two of Miriam's uncles are killed in the struggle for freedom. The baases simply say, "We do not intend to get upset by what is being said in all ignorance in the outside world."

Her voice is small, too, like a
nightingale's. But as she thinks about
her mother, her family, her people, she
finds strength.

"I appeal to you, to all the countries of
the world, to do everything you can to
stop the coming tragedy."

Her song becomes so strong
that she is invited to the United
Nations to speak about South
Africa. From this stage, she can
tell the whole world!

The whole world is listening.
Miriam feels very small in the
giant building.

But the outside world is no longer ignorant. They start listening to Miriam's songs. She sings to her people to be brave. *"Jolinkomo!"* She sings of police raids. *"Khawuleza!"* She sings of her people being jailed. *"Lakutshona Ilanga!"* She sends them strength with her song.

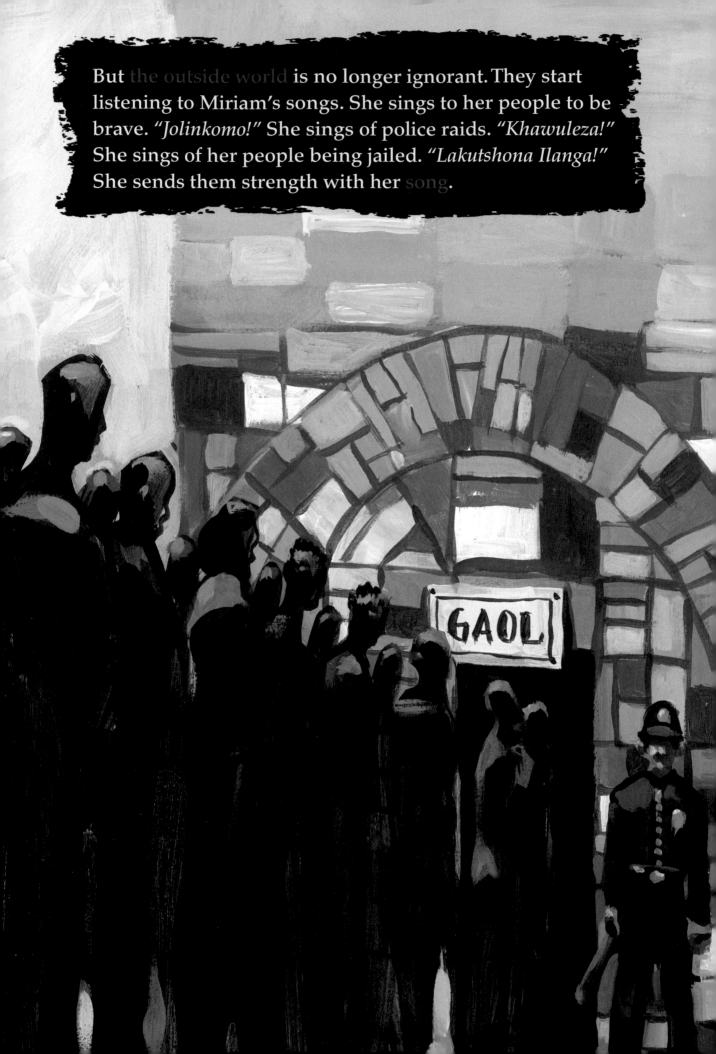

The baases pass more laws to stop people from protesting. They arrest thousands and jail many. Two of Miriam's uncles are killed in the struggle for freedom. The baases simply say, "We do not intend to get upset by what is being said in all ignorance in the outside world."

"Home? South Africa is no longer your home," the baases tell her. If she ever tries to return to her country, they will put her in jail. Even when she finds out her mother is sick, the baases will not let her back in.

In tears, Miriam sings. "*Senzeni na? What have we done?*" She knows her people have done nothing to deserve what the baases do to them. She stays in America and turns her tears into songs against the baases.

"Beware, Verwoerd!" she sings back to the prime minister. *"Ndodemnyama!"* To escape South Africa, Miriam disguises herself in a nanny uniform and boards a plane bound for Europe. For the first time in her life, she is free of apartheid! She sings in London and Los Angeles and New York about what the baases are doing to her people.

But she cannot sing too loudly. Her whole family is still in South Africa. What will the baases do to her people back home?

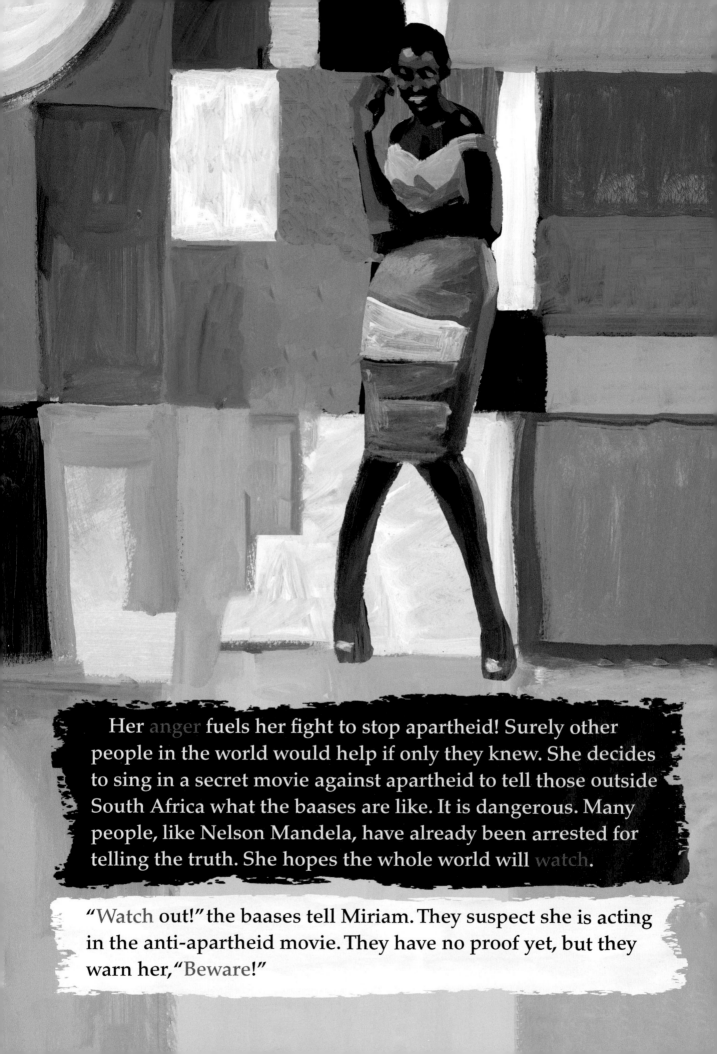

Her anger fuels her fight to stop apartheid! Surely other people in the world would help if only they knew. She decides to sing in a secret movie against apartheid to tell those outside South Africa what the baases are like. It is dangerous. Many people, like Nelson Mandela, have already been arrested for telling the truth. She hopes the whole world will watch.

"Watch out!" the baases tell Miriam. They suspect she is acting in the anti-apartheid movie. They have no proof yet, but they warn her, "Beware!"

Help comes, but the ambulance takes only the people in the other car. They are white. Miriam's friend, Victor, is black. By the time Miriam finds help, Victor is dead.

"Dead? Why did this man have to die?" she sings. "*Ityala lamadoda!*" Miriam is so angry.

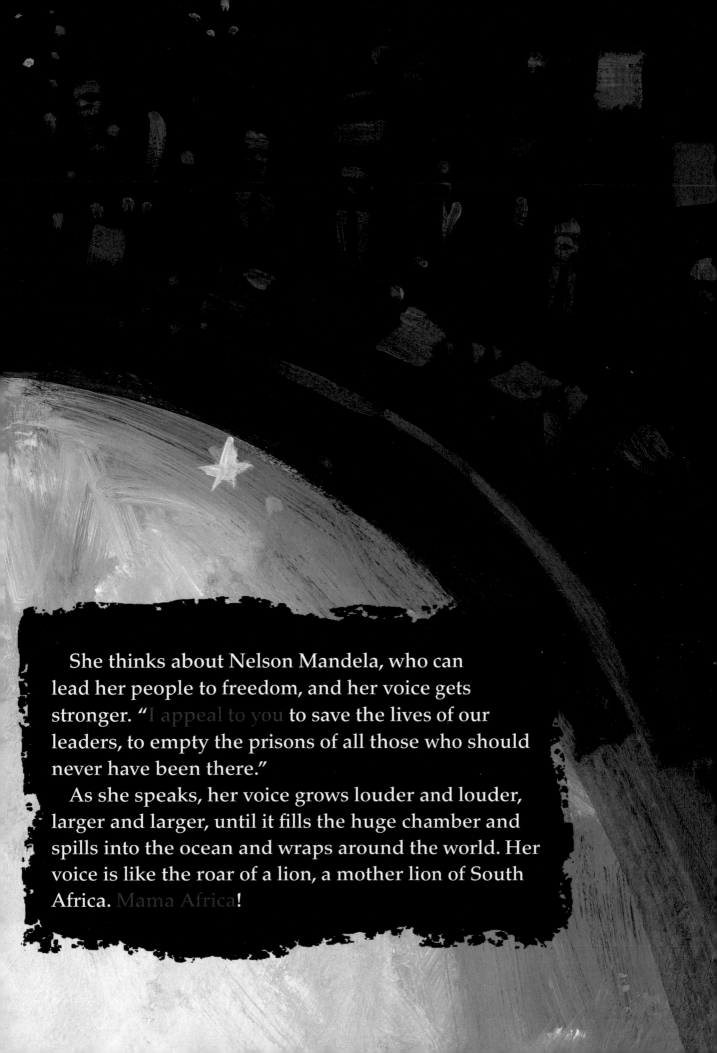

She thinks about Nelson Mandela, who can lead her people to freedom, and her voice gets stronger. "I appeal to you to save the lives of our leaders, to empty the prisons of all those who should never have been there."

As she speaks, her voice grows louder and louder, larger and larger, until it fills the huge chamber and spills into the ocean and wraps around the world. Her voice is like the roar of a lion, a mother lion of South Africa. Mama Africa!

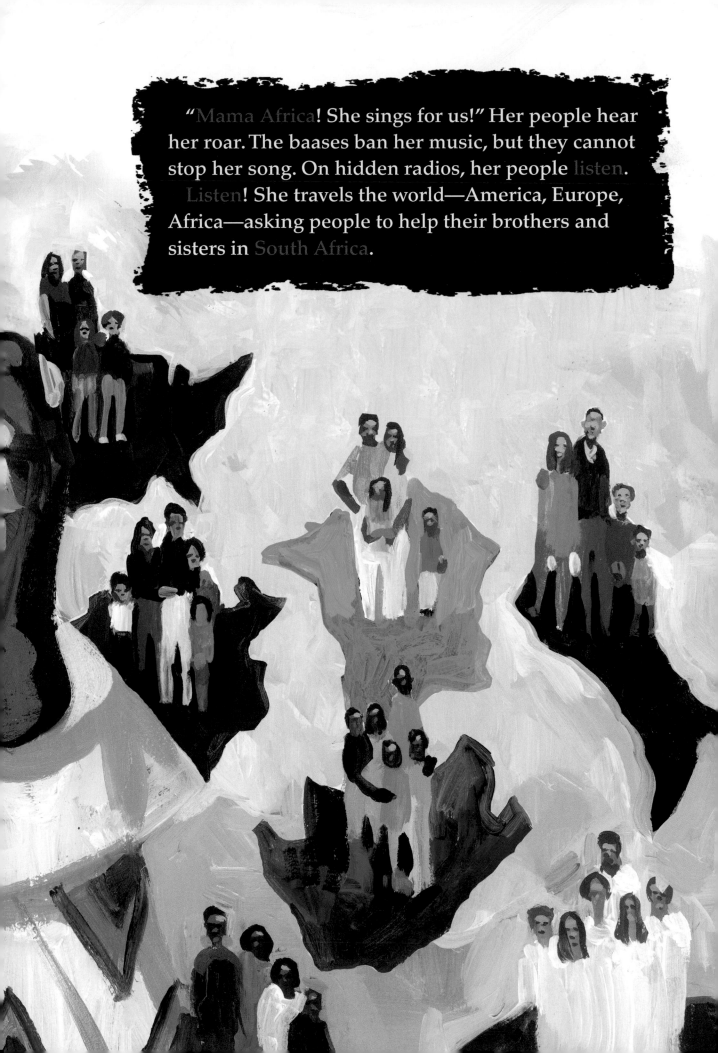

"Mama Africa! She sings for us!" Her people hear her roar. The baases ban her music, but they cannot stop her song. On hidden radios, her people listen. Listen! She travels the world—America, Europe, Africa—asking people to help their brothers and sisters in South Africa.

South Africans, many of them, both black and white, protest apartheid—marching, striking, speaking, writing. Some black protesters must flee the baases. They go to northern Africa and find Mama Africa.

Mama Africa helps the refugees—young men and women, even children. She gives them food, clothes, and song. When her song becomes too loud for some, they say she is not a singer but a politician. "I am no politician," she says. "I just see what I think is wrong and what is right."

And then something very wrong happens that shows the world Mama Africa is right. In the township of Soweto, schoolchildren protest being taught in Afrikaans, the language of apartheid. They are peaceful. They are unarmed. But the police shoot and kill many of them—children! The world is horrified.

Horrified, Mama Africa watches as protests continue, children are jailed, and her people fall one by one, beaten down.

She rises up with her song "Soweto Blues"!
Musicians around the world follow with their
songs: "It's Wrong," "Johannesburg," "Free Nelson
Mandela."

Nelson Mandela is still in prison. Mama Africa
must be his voice and keep his people strong.
More and more—black, white, Asian, people of all
races—join anti-apartheid groups in South Africa.
Allies around the world join her song.

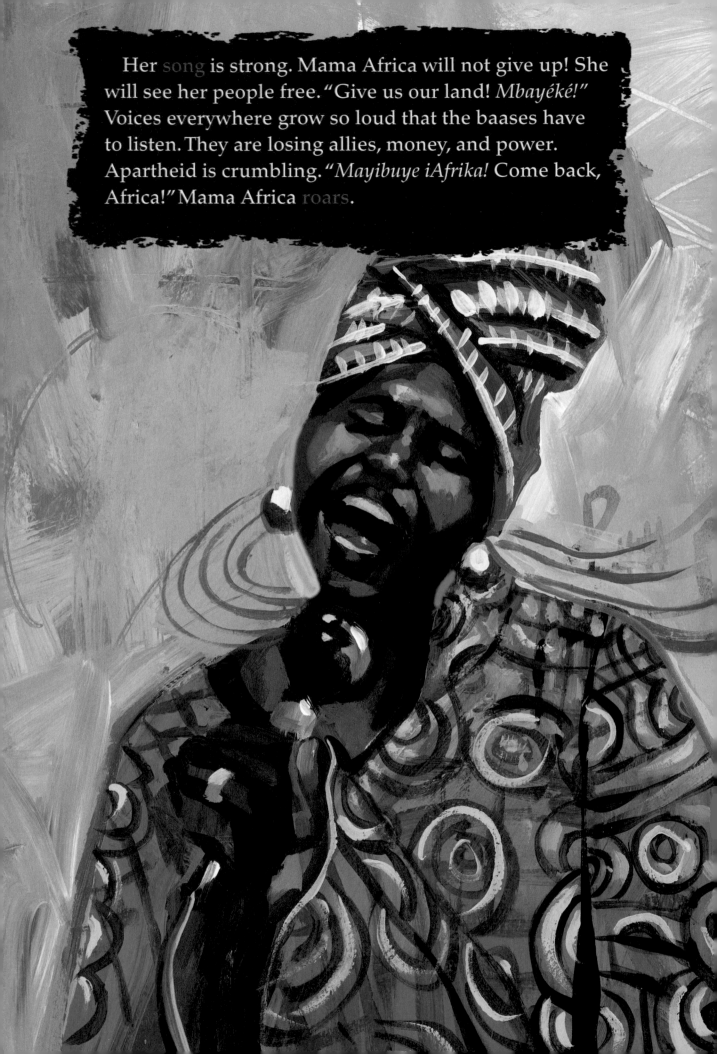

Her song is strong. Mama Africa will not give up! She will see her people free. "Give us our land! *Mbayéké!*" Voices everywhere grow so loud that the baases have to listen. They are losing allies, money, and power. Apartheid is crumbling. "*Mayibuye iAfrika!* Come back, Africa!" Mama Africa roars.

Mandela hears her roar. He says he will help the baases find a way to end apartheid and share the country equally. The baases must finally face the truth: all people of South Africa must have their freedom.

Freedom! Mama Africa watches Mandela walk out of prison. She watches the laws of apartheid fall one by one. And she sees her people stand tall. She sings with joy! Finally, her people are free!

"Free at last!" Mandela cries, and the crowds cheer. Now everyone in South Africa is free. Now everyone can go where they want, live where they want, and be who they want. Now Mama Africa can come home.

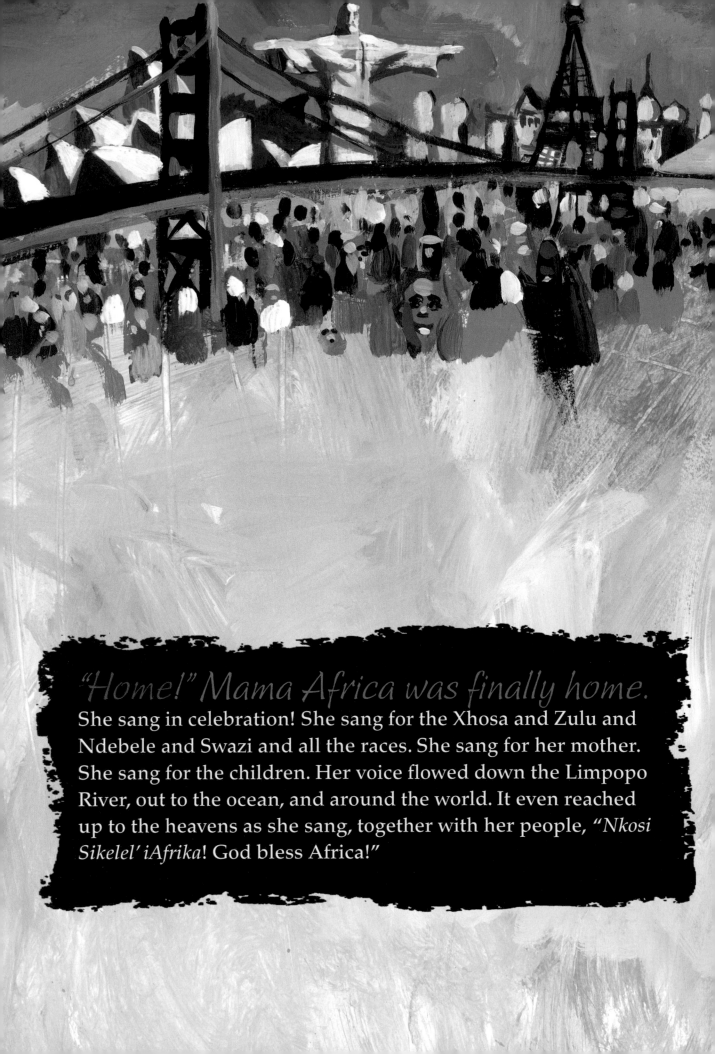

"Home!" Mama Africa was finally home.
She sang in celebration! She sang for the Xhosa and Zulu and
Ndebele and Swazi and all the races. She sang for her mother.
She sang for the children. Her voice flowed down the Limpopo
River, out to the ocean, and around the world. It even reached
up to the heavens as she sang, together with her people, *"Nkosi
Sikelel' iAfrika*! God bless Africa!"

AUTHOR'S NOTE

I wanted to write a biography of Miriam Makeba for children because I was introduced to her powerful music when I was a child. My family lived in South Africa for several years, and it was there that I first became aware of this strong and influential woman whose life and works would go on to make a deep impression on me. I hope that through reading her story you can understand that, even in the face of great odds, you always have a voice and your voice is powerful.

Note: All quotations in this section come from Miriam Makeba's two autobiographies, *Makeba: My Story* and *Makeba: The Miriam Makeba Story.*

The author (far right) with friend Theophilus, her sister, and Theophilus's sister, in the front yard of the author's home in Johannesburg, South Africa, 1964.

"I know a lot about our culture, our traditions and our traditional songs—thanks to my mother."

Miriam Makeba's music was banned in South Africa when I lived there as a child, but my mother played her records anyway, and we danced to her songs.

"Everything was separate. That is what the word 'apartheid' means."

My mother explained the policy of apartheid to me as best she could: There were no South African children of color at my school because they had separate schools, or none at all. White people wanted to control the country, so they created harsh laws to keep their nonwhite neighbors in fear and poverty. And although our family did not believe in this system, we were guests in South Africa and couldn't change their laws.

"Who can keep us down as long as we have our music?"

What we *could* do was treat all people with respect and as equals. And dance to banned music, played loudly. There was something rebellious and transcending about dancing to Miriam's music in our little living room in suburban Johannesburg.

"I am no politician. I just see what I think is wrong and what is right."

Even in my very privileged position, I felt constricted, confined, and deprived by apartheid. When I did have the chance to play with children of color, some white children would no longer play with me. It wasn't that I minded losing them as playmates; I just couldn't understand why they would shun an entire group of potential friends—new kids with new games, new music. It was clear to me that white people were also limiting themselves with apartheid, whether they realized it or not.

"One day, when they open that lid, you will see what will come out of the pot called South Africa."

The author with fellow students at Sandown Primary School, Johannesburg, South Africa, 1965.

Once, my sister was injured and I ran screaming for help. It was a black man who came to our aid. He carried her, racing to find a white family to drive her to the hospital since he himself was not allowed to drive. I waited into the night to see if she'd survive (she did), horrified by both her fate and a regime that treated a grown man like a child. What if she'd bled to death just because a black man wasn't given a license unless a white person said he could have one? What if we had been black children? People, I realized, could literally die because of this discrimination.

"Our lives had no value . . . But our people would no longer sit back either."

For people of color, life in South Africa was horrifying on a daily basis, and people did literally die. Miriam Makeba grew up in a loving extended family, surrounded by music. But she was also practically penniless and powerless, living in fear of saying or doing something deemed wrong. Two of her uncles were killed in the Sharpeville massacre. Other friends and colleagues were killed or disappeared, never to be seen again, during the apartheid regime.

"I was angry but I was grateful to be given a platform to voice my feelings."

Miriam sang from an early age, and she sang well. She used her talent to make money for her family. Sometimes she sang songs in native South African languages so the government could not understand the protest messages in the lyrics.

"Through my music I became this voice and image of Africa and the people without even realizing it."

When she became more outspoken and popular and traveled to Europe and America to sing, the South African government revoked her citizenship as punishment. She came to live in the United States and performed for famous movie stars and President John F. Kennedy, as well as for citizens and social activists, attending civil rights rallies alongside the Reverend Martin Luther King, Jr.

"I called for the world to take action against South Africa, a country that had been turned into a nightmare for blacks."

Miriam moved from country to country, always singing and performing. Everywhere she went, she sang about the plight of her people—and others who were oppressed. It was not an easy life in exile. Often, she was ignored or criticized.

The author helping to hold a political meeting sign for the anti-apartheid Social Democratic Party in Swaziland, 1964.

"If you wish for something and it doesn't happen,
you must hang on for dear life until it does."

What inspires me about Miriam Makeba is her resilience, her refusal to give up, and her unfailing dedication to her people, which drove her to battle impossible odds. I have often thought: If she could do it, why can't we all use our voices, our song, to confront the thinly veiled apartheid of the United States and inhumane treatment anywhere in the world?

"There are three things I was born with . . . hope, determination, and song."

As different as we were, Miriam and my mother and I shared some connections: being women, especially when women's rights were limited; being small and shy until we found our own voices; moving from country to country; being mothers; surviving cancer; and believing fiercely in treating people with respect and as equals. When I lost my mother, I passed Miriam's music and, I hope, her spirit on to my own children. And just like I had with my mother, we danced in the living room to Miriam's songs.

"I had hope. Our people did not give up."

Music unites us all. The power of song is an intangible force that gives us strength. Lyrics have meaning and power, and music connects us emotionally and spiritually to people elsewhere on Earth. That magical transcending force called empathy can eventually help change the world. It has. And it still can.

SELECTED BIBLIOGRAPHY

Books

Bordowitz, Hank. *Noise of the World: Non-Western Musicians in Their Own Words*. Brooklyn, N.Y.: Soft Skull Press, 2004.

Burns, Rebecca. *Burial for a King*. New York: Scribner, 2011.

Feldstein, Ruth. *How It Feels to Be Free: Black Women Entertainers and the Civil Rights Movement*. New York: Oxford University Press, 2013.

Ford, Tanisha C. *Liberated Threads: Black Women, Style, and the Global Politics of Soul*. Chapel Hill, N.C.: University of North Carolina, 2015.

Makeba, Miriam. *The World of African Song*. Chicago: Quadrangle, 1971.

Makeba, Miriam, with James Hall. *Makeba: My Story*. New York: New American Library, 1987.

Makeba, Miriam, with Nomsa Mwamuka. *Makeba: The Miriam Makeba Story*. Johannesburg, South Africa: STE Publishers, 2004.

Schwarz-Bart, Simone, with André Schwarz-Bart. *In Praise of Black Women, Vol. 3: Modern African Women*. Madison, Wis.: University of Wisconsin Press, 2003.

Audio and Video Recordings

Amandla! A Revolution in Four-Part Harmony, Lions Gate B0000C2IWO, 2003, DVD.

An Evening with Belafonte/Makeba, RCA Victor Europe B00004SNG7, 1990, compact disc. Originally released in 1965.

Homeland, Putumayo B01AXM8TL6, 2000, compact disc.

In Concert! / Pata Pata / Makeba! Collectables B00007BH7J, 2002, compact disc. Originally released in 1967, 1967, and 1968, respectively.

Sarafina!, Echo Bridge Home Entertainment B004SUDQ3Q, 2011, DVD. Originally released in 1992.

FURTHER READING

Picture Books

Cooper, Floyd. *Mandela: From the Life of the South African Statesman*. New York: Puffin Books, 2000.

King, Martin Luther, Jr. *I Have a Dream*. Illustrated by Kadir Nelson. New York: Schwartz & Wade Books, 2012.

Levy, Debbie. *We Shall Overcome: The Story of a Song*. Illustrated by Vanessa Brantley-Newton. New York: Disney/Jump at the Sun Books, 2013.

Mandela, Nelson. *Long Walk to Freedom: Nelson Mandela*. Abridged by Chris Van Wyk. Illustrated by Paddy Bouma. New York: Roaring Brook Press, 2009.

Pinkney, Andrea Davis. *Ella Fitzgerald: The Tale of a Vocal Virtuosa*. Illustrated by Jerry Pinkney. New York: Hyperion, 2002.

Sisulu, Elinor Batezat. *The Day Gogo Went to Vote: South Africa, April 1994*. Illustrated by Sharon Wilson. Boston: Little, Brown, 1996.

Tonatiuh, Duncan. *Separate Is Never Equal: Sylvia Mendez and Her Family's Fight for Desegregation*. New York: Abrams Books for Young Readers, 2014.

Weatherford, Carole Boston. *Voice of Freedom: Fannie Lou Hamer, Spirit of the Civil Rights Movement*. Illustrated by Ekua Holmes. Somerville, Mass.: Candlewick Press, 2015.

Wulfsohn, Gisèle. *Bongani's Day: From Dawn to Dusk in a South African City*. London: Frances Lincoln Children's Books, 2011.

For Older Readers

Levine, Ellen. *If You Lived at the Time of Martin Luther King*. Illustrated by Anna Rich. New York: Scholastic, 1994.

Lewis, John, and Andrew Aydin. The March Trilogy. Illustrated by Nate Powell. Marietta, Ga.: Top Shelf Productions, 2013.

Lowery, Lynda Blackmon. *Turning 15 on the Road to Freedom: My Story of the Selma Voting Rights March*. Illustrated by PJ Loughran. New York: Dial Books, 2015.

Rappaport, Doreen. *Nobody Gonna Turn Me 'Round: Stories and Songs of the Civil Rights Movement*. Illustrated by Shane W. Evans. Cambridge, Mass.: Candlewick, 2008.

Weatherford, Carole Boston. *Becoming Billie Holiday*. Illustrated by Floyd Cooper. Honesdale, Pa.: Wordsong, 2008.

MAJOR EVENTS IN THE PUBLIC LIFE OF MIRIAM MAKEBA, THE ANTI-APARTHEID MOVEMENT, AND THE AMERICAN CIVIL RIGHTS ERA

1932   Zenzile Miriam Makeba is born on March 4, in Prospect Township, South Africa, near Johannesburg.

1948   Apartheid begins in South Africa.

1950   The Population Registration Act and the Group Areas Act are passed in South Africa to register each person's race and segregate residential areas. In response, Nelson Mandela leads a campaign of civil disobedience.

c. 1953   Miriam joins the singing group Manhattan Brothers.

c. 1954   Comedian Victor Mkhize, a man in a group Miriam performs with, dies after a car accident when he is refused access to a whites-only ambulance and hospital.

1957   Martin Luther King, Jr., becomes chairman of the nonviolent anti-segregation organization eventually known as the Southern Christian Leadership Conference (SCLC).

1959   Miriam performs in the anti-apartheid film *Come Back, Africa*.
She arrives in New York City with the help of performer and mentor Harry Belafonte.

1960   Miriam's South African passport and citizenship are revoked.
Dozens of black South Africans, including two of Miriam's uncles, are killed in the Sharpeville massacre while protesting apartheid.

1961   Miriam and Harry Belafonte perform in a SCLC benefit concert in Nashville, Tennessee, to support Martin Luther King, Jr., and the civil rights movement.

1962   Miriam and Harry Belafonte appear with Martin Luther King, Jr., at an SCLC benefit in Atlanta, Georgia.
Nelson Mandela is arrested.
Miriam tours Africa and South America to promote her music and deliver her anti-apartheid message.

1963   Martin Luther King, Jr., is arrested and writes "Letter from Birmingham Jail."
Nelson Mandela is sentenced to life in prison on Robben Island.
Miriam addresses the United Nations, requesting the release of leaders like Mandela as well as the world's assistance in dismantling apartheid.
South Africa bans her music.

1964   The United States passes the Civil Rights Act, which prohibits racial discrimination and segregation in education, employment, and public places.

1965   The United States passes the Voting Rights Act, protecting the rights of African Americans to vote.
Miriam appears with Martin Luther King, Jr., at a rally in New York City.
Miriam wins a Grammy Award for *An Evening with Belafonte/Makeba*.

1966   James Meredith is shot on his "March Against Fear," a walk from Memphis, Tennessee, to Jackson, Mississippi, to encourage African Americans in the South to register to vote. While he is hospitalized, his march is continued by, among others, Martin Luther King, Jr., and Stokely Carmichael.
Stokely Carmichael (later known as Kwame Ture), a leader of the Student Nonviolent Coordinating Committee (SNCC), coins the term "black power."

1967   Miriam meets Stokely Carmichael while visiting Guinea on an African tour.

1968   Martin Luther King, Jr., is assassinated; Miriam and Stokely Carmichael attend his funeral and walk in the procession together.
Miriam marries Stokely Carmichael, triggering a lack of interest in her performances in the United States because of his status as a "radical."

1969	Miriam and Stokely Carmichael move to Guinea, where Miriam joins the Guinean delegation to the United Nations.
1970	The Bantu Homelands Citizenship Act passes in South Africa, revoking the citizenship of black Africans and allowing their forcible removal to artificial "homelands."
1970s	Miriam continues touring Africa, South America, the Caribbean, Europe, the Middle East, and the United States, singing and raising awareness about apartheid.
1976	Miriam addresses the United Nations again, urging the world to support the fight against apartheid and atrocities like the Sharpeville massacre.
1976–77	Thousands of black South Africans, including some schoolchildren, are killed in the Soweto student uprising and subsequent countrywide protests objecting to the use of Afrikaans in schools and the policy of apartheid.
1977	The Sullivan Principles are adopted by a dozen major U.S. corporations with investments in South Africa. The signees would demand that South African companies give equal treatment to their white and nonwhite employees.
1980s	Miriam continues touring Africa and the world, spreading her anti-apartheid message.
1986	The Comprehensive Anti-Apartheid Act passes in the United States, limiting the business companies can do with South Africa.
1987–89	Miriam accompanies Paul Simon on his *Graceland* world tour, as well as continuing to tour for her own music and to speak out against apartheid.
1990	Nelson Mandela is freed from prison. Miriam is allowed to return to South Africa after thirty years in exile.
1991	The four primary apartheid laws are repealed, initiating its demise.
1992	Miriam stars in *Sarafina!*, a film about the Soweto uprising.
1993	The Interim Constitution affords equal rights to all South Africans.
1994	South Africa holds its first election for all races and Nelson Mandela is elected president. Miriam votes for the first time in her life, at age sixty-two.
1996	South Africa begins Truth and Reconciliation Commission hearings on human rights violations committed during apartheid.
1997	A new constitution is adopted in South Africa, including a Bill of Rights.
1999	Miriam is named Goodwill Ambassador by the Food and Agriculture Organization of the United Nations.
2001	Miriam's album *Homeland* is nominated for a Grammy Award. Miriam is appointed South Africa's Goodwill Ambassador to Africa.
2002	Miriam stars in *Amandla! A Revolution in Four-Part Harmony*, a documentary celebrating how music served as a powerful form of protest and unification in the anti-apartheid movement.
2008	Miriam dies on November 10 following a concert in Italy in support of Roberto Saviano, an Italian journalist who had received death threats for exposing a crime syndicate in Naples, and in memory of six immigrants from Africa killed by that group.

GLOSSARY

Here is a list of foreign words and phrases used in this book, along with their basic definitions and pronunciations.

Afrikaans (*Ahf-ree-kahnz*): one of the eleven official languages of South Africa. It developed from Dutch in the seventeenth century.

apartheid (*ah-par-tide*): in South Africa, a systemic policy of segregation leading to political and economic discrimination against nonwhite peoples. In general, racial segregation.

baas (*bahs*): boss or master; often used by nonwhites in southern Africa when speaking about or to white people in positions of power.

Bantu (*bahn-too*): describing or relating to a group of Niger-Congo languages spoken in central and southern Africa. During apartheid, it became a derogatory word to describe native African peoples.

isiXhosa (*ee-see Koh-zah*): an official language of South Africa, and the language of the Xhosa people. It is also part of the Bantu language group. Nearly 20% of the South African population speaks isiXhosa.

isiZulu (*ee-see Zoo-loo*): an official language of South Africa, and the language of the Zulu people. It is the second-most-common Bantu language, spoken by nearly 25% of South Africans.

"Ityala Lamadoda" (*Ee-tyah-lah Lah-mah-doh-dah*): a Xhosa song honoring those killed or imprisoned during apartheid; most likely refers to Henry Nxumalo, an investigative journalist, and comedian Victor Mkize, Miriam's friend who died after a car accident.

"Jolinkomo" (*Joh-lin-koh-moh*): a Xhosa folk song Miriam sang that encourages warriors to be brave in battle.

"Khawuleza" (*Kah-woo-lay-zah*): a Xhosa song in which children in townships warn their mothers that the police are coming.

"Lakutshona Ilanga" (*Lah-koot-show-nah Ee-lahn-gah*): a Xhosa song about searching for missing loved ones in hospitals and jails.

"Mayibuye iAfrika" (*My-yee-boo-yeh ee-Ahf-ree-kah*): a Xhosa song calling for the return of Africa to native Africans.

"Mbayéké" (*Ehm-buy-yeh-keh*): a Zulu song demanding one's land back.

Ndebele (*Ehn-deh-bee-lee*): an ethnic group primarily from two provinces in northeastern South Africa.

"Ndodemnyama" (*Ehn-doh-dem-nyah-mah*): a Xhosa song telling the South African government to beware because apartheid will soon crumble.

"Nkosi Sikelel' iAfrika" (*Ehn-koh-see See-keh-leh-lee Ahf-ree-kah*): one of the two hymns that combined make up the South African national anthem, with verses in isiXhosa, isiZulu, Sesotho, Afrikaans, and English, meaning "God bless Africa."

"Senzeni Na" (*Sen-zen-ee Nah*): a song in isiXhosa and isiZulu asking "What have we done?" to question why black people in South Africa are treated so badly.

Setswana (*Set-swah-nah*): an official language of South Africa and Botswana, and the language of the Tswana people. It is also part of the Bantu language group. About 10% of South Africans speak Setswana.

Swazi (*Swah-zee*): the people of Swaziland, a sovereign state that shares a border with South Africa. Many Swazis live in South Africa.

Tswana (*Tswah-nah*): an ethnic group native to Botswana and South Africa.

"Umoya" (*Oo-moy-yah*): a Zulu song meaning "Spirit."

Verwoerd (*Fair-vert*)**, Hendrik**: a white, Dutch-born South African politician who developed and implemented apartheid. He was prime minister from 1958 until he was killed in 1966.

Xhosa (*Koh-zah*): an ethnic group primarily from the Eastern Cape province of South Africa. Both Miriam Makeba and Nelson Mandela were Xhosa.

Zulu (*Zoo-loo*): the largest ethnic group in South Africa, living mainly in the KwaZulu-Natal province.